Auguste Groner

The Case of the Pool of Blood in the Pastor's Study

Leseklassiker

Auguste Groner

The Case of the Pool of Blood in the Pastor's Study

ISBN/EAN: 9783955630300

Auflage: 1

Erscheinungsjahr: 2013

Erscheinungsort: Bremen, Deutschland

Contents

INTRODUCTION TO JOE MULLER

Joseph Muller, Secret Service detective of the Imperial Austrian police, is one of the great experts in his profession. In personality he differs greatly from other famous detectives. He has neither the impressive authority of Sherlock Holmes, nor the keen brilliancy of Monsieur Lecoq. Muller is a small, slight, plain-looking man, of indefinite age, and of much humbleness of mien. A naturally retiring, modest disposition, and two external causes are the reasons for Muller's humbleness of manner, which is his chief characteristic. One cause is the fact that in early youth a miscarriage of justice gave him several years in prison, an experience which cast a stigma on his name and which made it impossible for him, for many years after, to obtain honest employment. But the world is richer, and safer, by Muller's early misfortune. For it was this experience which threw him back on his own peculiar talents for a livelihood, and drove him into the police force. Had he been able to enter any other profession, his genius might have been stunted to a mere pastime, instead of being, as now, utilised for the public good.

Then, the red tape and bureaucratic etiquette which attaches to every governmental department, puts the secret service men of the Imperial police on a par with the lower ranks of the subordinates. Muller's official rank is scarcely much higher than that of a policeman, although kings and councillors consult him and the Police Department realises to the full what a treasure it has in him. But official red tape, and his early misfortune... prevent the giving of any higher official standing to even such a genius. Born and bred to such conditions, Muller understands them, and his natural modesty of disposition asks for no outward honours, asks for nothing but an income sufficient for his simple needs, and for aid and opportunity to occupy himself in the way he most enjoys.

Joseph Muller's character is a strange mixture. The kindest-hearted man in the world, he is a human bloodhound when once the lure of the trail has caught him. He scarcely eats or sleeps when the chase is on, he does not seem to know human weakness nor fatigue, in spite of his frail body. Once put on a case his mind delves and delves until it finds a clue, then something awakes within him, a spirit akin to that which holds the bloodhound nose to trail, and he will accomplish the apparently impossible, he will track down his victim when the entire machinery of a great police department seems helpless to discover anything. The high chiefs and commissioners grant a condescending permission when Muller asks, "May I do this? ... or may I handle this case this way?" both parties knowing all the while that it is a farce, and that the department waits helpless until this humble little man saves its honour by solving some problem before which its intricate machinery has stood dazed and puzzled.

This call of the trail is something that is stronger than anything else in Muller's mentality, and now and then it brings him into conflict with the department,... or with his own better nature. Sometimes his unerring instinct discovers secrets in high places, secrets which the Police Department is bidden to hush up and leave untouched. Muller is then taken off the case, and left idle for a while if he persists in his opinion as to the true facts. And at other times, Muller's own warm heart gets him into trouble. He will track down his victim, driven by the power in his soul which is stronger than all volition; but when he has this victim in the net, he will sometimes discover him to be a much finer, better man than the other individual, whose wrong at this particular criminal's hand set in motion the machinery of justice. Several times that has happened to Muller, and each time his heart got the better of his professional instincts, of his practical common-sense, too, perhaps,... at least as far as his own advancement was concerned, and he warned the victim, defeating his own work. This peculiarity of Muller's character caused his undoing at last, his official undoing that is, and compelled his retirement from the force. But his advice is often sought unofficially by the Department, and to those who know, Muller's hand can be seen in the unravelling of many a famous case.

The following stories are but a few of the

many interesting cases that have come within the experience of this great detective. But they give a fair portrayal of Muller's peculiar method of working, his looking on himself as merely an humble member of the Department, and the comedy of his acting under "official orders" when the Department is in reality following out his directions.

THE CASE OF THE POOL OF BLOOD IN THE PASTOR'S STUDY

The sun rose slowly over the great bulk of the Carpathian mountains lying along the horizon, weird giant shapes in the early morning mist. It was still very quiet in the village. A cock crowed here and there, and swallows flew chirping close to the ground, darting swiftly about preparing for their higher flight. Janci the shepherd, apparently the only human being already up, stood beside the brook at the point where the old bridge spans the streamlet, still turbulent from the mountain floods. Janci was cutting willows to make his Margit a new basket.

Once the shepherd raised his head from his work, for he thought he heard a loud laugh somewhere in the near distance. But all seemed silent and he turned back to his willows. The beauty of the landscape about him was much too familiar a thing that he should have felt or seen its charm. The violet hue of the distant woods, the red gleaming of the heather-strewn moor, with its patches of swamp from which the slow mist arose, the pretty little village with its handsome old church and attractive rectory — Janci had known it so long that he never stopped to realise how very charming, in its gentle melancholy, it all was.

Also, Janci did not know that this little village of his home had once been a flourishing city, and that an invasion of the Turks had razed it to the ground leaving, as by a miracle, only the church to tell of former glories.

The sun rose higher and higher. And now the village awoke to its daily life. Voices of cattle and noises of poultry were heard about the houses, and men and women began their accustomed round of tasks. Janci found that he had gathered enough willow twigs by this time. He tied them in a loose bundle and started on his homeward way.

His path led through wide-stretching fields and vineyards past a little hill, some distance from the village, on which stood a large house. It was not a pleasant house to look at, not a house one would care to live in, even if one did not know its use, for it looked bare and repellant, covered with its ugly yellow paint, and with all the windows secured with heavy iron bars. The trees that surrounded it were tall and thick-foliaged, casting an added gloom over the forbidding appearance of the house. At the foot of the hill was a high iron fence, cutting off what lay behind it from all the rest of the world. For this ugly yellow house enclosed in its walls a goodly sum of hopeless human misery and misfortune. It was an insane asylum.

For twenty years now, the asylum had stood on its hill, a source of superstitious terror to the villagers, but at the same time a source of added income. It meant money for them, for it afforded a constant and ever-open market for their farm products and the output of their home industry. But every now and then a scream or a harsh laugh would ring out from behind those barred windows, and those in the village who could hear, would shiver and cross themselves. Shepherd Janci had little fear of the big house. His little hut cowered close by the high iron gates, and he had a personal acquaintance with most of the patients, with all of the attendants, and most of all, with the kind elderly physician who was the head of the establishment. Janci knew them all, and had a kind word equally for all. But otherwise he was a silent man, living much within himself.

When the shepherd reached his little home, his wife came to meet him with a call to breakfast. As they sat down at the table a shadow moved past the little window. Janci looked up. "Who was that?" asked Margit, looking up from her folded hands. She had just finished her murmured prayer.

"Pastor's Liska," replied Janci indifferently, beginning his meal. (Liska was the local abbreviation for Elizabeth.)'

"In such a hurry?" thought the shepherd's wife. Her curiosity would not let her rest. "I hope His Reverence isn't ill again," she remarked after a while. Janci did not hear her, for he was very busy picking a fly out of his milk cup.

"Do you think Liska was going for the old man?" began Margit again after a few minutes.

The "old man" was the name given by the people of the village, more as a term of endearment than anything else, to the generally loved and respected physician who was the head of the insane asylum. He had become general mentor and oracle of all the village and was known and loved by man, woman and child.

"It's possible," answered Janci.

"His Reverence didn't look very well yesterday, or maybe the old housekeeper has the gout again."

Janci gave a grunt which might have meant anything. The shepherd was a silent man. Being alone so much had taught him to find his own thoughts sufficient company. Ten minutes passed in silence since Margit's last question, then some one went past the window. There were two people this time, Liska and the old doctor. They were walking very fast, running almost. Margit sprang up and hurried to the door to look after them.

Janci sat still in his place, but he had laid aside his spoon and with wide eyes was staring ahead of him, murmuring, "It's the pastor this time; I saw him — just as I did the others."

"Shepherd, the inn-keeper wants to see you, there's something the matter with his cow." Count — — a young man, coming from the other direction and pushing in at the door past Margit, who stood there staring up the road.

Janci was so deep in his own thoughts that he apparently did not hear the boy's words. At all events he did not answer them, but himself asked an unexpected question — a question that was not addressed to the others in the room, but to something out and beyond them. It was a strange question and it came from the lips of a man whose mind was not with his body at that moment — whose mind saw what others did not see.

"Who will be the next to go? And who will be our pastor now?"

These were Janci's words.

"What are you talking about, shepherd? Is it another one of your visions?" exclaimed the young fellow who stood there before him. Janci rubbed his hands over his eyes and seemed to come down to earth with a start.

"Oh, is that you, Ferenz? What do you want of me?"

The boy gave his message again, and Janci nodded good-humouredly and followed him out of the house. But both he and his young companion were very thoughtful as they plodded along the way. The boy did not dare to ask any questions, for he knew that the shepherd was not likely to answer. There was a silent understanding among the villagers that no one should annoy

Janci in any way, for they stood in a strange awe of him, although he was the most good-natured mortal under the sun.

While the shepherd and the boy walked toward the inn, the old doctor and Liska had hurried onward to the rectory. They were met at the door by the aged housekeeper, who staggered down the path wringing her hands, unable to give voice to anything but inarticulate expressions of grief and terror. The rest of the household and the farm hands were gathered in a frightened group in the great courtyard of the stately rectory which had once been a convent building. The physician hurried up the stairs into the pastor's apartments. These were high sunny and airy rooms with arched ceilings, deep window seats, great heavy doors and handsomely ornamented stoves. The simple modern furniture appeared still more plain and common-place by contrast with the huge spaces of the building.

In one of the rooms a gendarme was standing beside the window. The man saluted the physician, then shrugged his shoulders with an expression of hopelessness. The doctor returned a silent greeting and passed through into the next apartment. The old man was paler than usual and his face bore an expression of pain and surprise, the same expression that showed in the faces of those gathered downstairs. The room he now entered was large like the others, the walls handsomely decorated, and every corner of it was flooded with sunshine. There were two men in this room, the village magistrate and the notary. Their expression, as they held out their hands to the doctor, showed that his coming brought great relief. And there was something else in the room, something that drew the eyes of all three of the men immediately after their silent greeting.

This was a great pool of blood which lay as a hideous stain on the otherwise clean yellow-painted floor. The blood must have flowed from a dreadful wound, from a severed artery even, the doctor thought, there was such a quantity of it. It had already dried and darkened, making its terrifying ugliness the more apparent.

"This is the third murder in two years," said the magistrate in a low voice.

"And the most mysterious of all of them," added the clerk.

"Yes, it is," said the doctor. "And there is not a trace of the body, you say? — or a clue as to where they might have taken the dead — or dying man?"

With these words he looked carefully around the room, but there was no more blood to be seen anywhere. Any spot would have been clearly visible on the light-coloured floor. There was nothing else to tell of the horrible crime that had been committed here, nothing but the great, hideous, brown-red spot in the middle of the room.

"Have you made a thorough search for the body?" asked the doctor.

The magistrate shook his head. "No, I have done nothing to speak of yet. We have been waiting for you. There is a gendarme at the gate; no one can go in or out without being seen."

"Very well, then, let us begin our search now."

The magistrate and his companion turned towards the door of the room but the doctor motioned them to come back. "I see you do not know the house as well as I do," he said, and led the way towards a niche in the side of the wall, which was partially filled by a high bookcase.

"Ah — that is the entrance of the passage to the church?" asked the magistrate in surprise.

"Yes, this is it. The door is not locked."

"You mean you believe — "

"That the murderers came in from the church? Why not? It is quite possible."

"To think of such a thing!" exclaimed the notary with a shake of his head.

The doctor laughed bitterly. "To those who are planning a murder, a church is no more than any other place. There is a bolt here as you see. I will close this bolt now. Then we can leave the room knowing that no one can enter it without being seen."

The simple furniture of the study, a desk, a sofa, a couple of chairs and several bookcases, gave no chance of any hiding place either for the body of the victim or for the murderers. When the men left the room the magistrate locked the door and put the key in his own pocket. The gendarme in the neighbouring apartment was sent down to stand in the courtyard at the entrance to the house. The sexton, a little hunchback, was ordered to remain in the vestry at the other end of the passage from the church to the house.

Then the thorough search of the house began. Every room in both stories, every corner of the attic and the cellar, was looked over thoroughly. The stable, the barns, the garden and even the well underwent a close examination. There was no trace of a body anywhere, not even a trail of blood, nothing which would give the slightest clue as to how the murderers had entered, how they had fled, or what they had done with their victim.

The great gate of the courtyard was closed. The men, reinforced by the farm hands, entered the church, while Liska and the dairy-maids huddled in the servants' dining-room in a trembling group around the old housekeeper. The search in the church as well as in the vestry was equally in vain. There was no trace to be found there any more than in the house.

Meanwhile, during these hours of anxious seeking, the rumour of another terrible crime had spread through the village, and a crowd that grew from minute to minute gathered in front of the closed gates to the rectory, in front of the church, the closed doors of which did not open although it was a high feast day. The utter silence from the steeple, where the bells hung mute, added to the spreading terror. Finally the doctor came out from the rectory, accompanied by the magistrate, and announced to the waiting villagers that their venerable pastor had disappeared under circumstances which left no doubt that he had met his death at the hand of a murderer. The peasants listened in shuddering silence, the men pale-faced, the women sobbing aloud with frightened children hanging to their skirts. Then at the magistrate's order, the crowd dispersed slowly, going to their homes, while a messenger set off to the near-by county seat.

It was a weird, sad Easter Monday. Even nature seemed to feel the pressure of the brooding horror, for heavy clouds piled up towards noon and a chill wind blew fitfully from the north, bending the young corn and the creaking tree-tops, and moaning about the straw-covered roofs. Then an icy cold rain descended on the village, sending the children, the only humans still unconscious of the fear that had come on them all, into the houses to play quietly in the corner by the hearth.

There was nothing else spoken of wherever two or three met together throughout the village except this dreadful, unexplainable thing that had happened in the rectory. The little village inn was full to overflowing and the hum of voices within was like the noise of an excited beehive. Everyone had some new explanation, some new guess, and it was not until the notary arrived, looking even more important than usual, that silence fell upon the excited throng. But the expectations aroused by his coming were not fulfilled. The notary knew no more than the others although he had been one of the searchers in the rectory. But he was in no haste to disclose his ignorance, and sat wrapped in a dignified silence until some one found courage to question him.

"Was there nothing stolen?" he was asked.

"No, nothing as far as we can tell yet. But if it was the gypsies — as may be likely — they are content with so little that it would not be noticed."

"Gypsies?" exclaimed one man scornfully. "It doesn't have to be gypsies, we've got enough tramps and vagabonds of our own. Didn't they kill the pedlar for the sake of a bag of tobacco, and old Katiza for a couple of hens?"

"Why do you rake up things that happened twenty years ago?" cried another over the table. "You'd better tell us rather who killed Red Betty, and pulled Janos, the smith's farm hand, down into the swamp?"

"Yes, or who cut the bridge supports, when

the brook was in flood, so that two good cows broke through and drowned?"

"Yes, indeed, if we only knew what band of robbers and villains it is that is ravaging our village."

"And they haven't stopped yet, evidently."

"This is the worst misfortune of all! What will our poor do now that they have murdered our good pastor, who cared for us all like a father?"

"He gave all he had to the poor, he kept nothing for himself."

"Yes, indeed, that's how it was. And now we can't even give this good man Christian burial."

"Shepherd Janci knew this morning early that we were going to have a new pastor," whispered the landlord in the notary's ear. The latter looked up astonished. "Who said so?" he asked.

"My boy Ferenz, who went to fetch him about seven o'clock. One of my cows was sick."

Ferenz was sent for and told his story. The men listened with great interest, and the smith, a broad-shouldered elderly man, was particularly eager to hear, as he had always believed in the shepherd's power of second sight. The tailor, who was more modern-minded, laughed and made his jokes at this. But the smith laid one mighty hand on the other's shoulder, almost crushing the tailor's slight form under its weight, and said gravely: "Friend, do you be silent in this matter. You've come from other parts and you do not know of things that have happened here in days gone by. Janci can do more than take care of his sheep. One day, when my little girl was playing in the street, he said to me, 'Have a care of Maruschka, smith!' and three days later the child was dead. The evening before Red Betty was murdered he saw her in a vision lying in a coffin in front of her door. He told it to the sexton, whom he met in the fields; and next morning they found Betty dead. And there are many more things that I could tell you, but what's the use; when a man won't believe it's only lost talk to try to make him. But one thing you should know: when Janci stares ahead of him without seeing what's in front of him, then the whole village begins to wonder what's going to happen, for Janci knows far more than all the rest of us put together."

The smith's grave, deep voice filled the room and the others listened in a silence that gave assent to his words. He had scarcely finished speaking, however, when there was a noise of galloping hoofs and rapidly rolling wagon wheels. A tall brake drawn by four handsome horses dashed past in a whirlwind.

"It's the Count — the Count and the district judge," said the landlord in a tone of respect. The notary made a grab at his hat and umbrella and hurried from the room. "That shows how much they thought of our pastor," continued the landlord proudly. "For the Count himself has come and with four horses, too, to get here the more quickly. His Reverence was a great friend of the Countess."

"They didn't make so much fuss over the pedlar and Betty," murmured the cobbler, who suffered from a perpetual grouch. But he followed the others, who paid their scores hastily and went out into the streets that they might watch from a distance at least what was going on in the rectory. The landlord bustled about the inn to have everything in readiness in case the gentlemen should honour him by taking a meal, and perhaps even lodgings, at his house. At the gate of the rectory the coachman and the maid Liska stood to receive the newcomers, just as five o'clock was striking from the steeple.

It should have been still quite light, but it was already dusk, for the clouds hung heavy. The rain had ceased, but a heavy wind came up which tore the delicate petals of the blossoms from the fruit trees and strewed them like snow on the ground beneath. The Count, who was the head of one of the richest and most aristocratic families in Hungary, threw off his heavy fur coat and hastened up the stairs at the top of which his old friend and confidant, the venerable pastor, usually came to meet him. To-day it was only the local magistrate who stood there, bowing deeply.

"This is incredible, incredible!" exclaimed the Count.

"It is, indeed, sir," said the man, leading the magnate through the dining-room into the pastor's study, where, as far as could be seen, the murder had been committed. They were joined by the district judge, who had remained behind to give an order sending a carriage to the nearest railway station. The judge, too, was serious and deeply shocked, for he also had greatly admired and revered the old pastor. The stately rectory had been the scene of many a jovial gathering when the lord of the manor had made it a centre for a day's hunting with his friends. The bearers of some of the proudest names in all Hungary had gathered in the high-arched rooms to laugh with the venerable pastor and to sample the excellent wines in his cellar. These wines, which the gentlemen themselves would send in as presents to the master of the rectory, would be carefully preserved for their own enjoyment. Not a landed proprietor for many leagues around but knew and loved the old pastor, who had now so strangely disappeared under such terrifying circumstances.

"Well, we might as well begin our examination," remarked the Count. "Although if Dr. Orszay's sharp eyes did not find anything, I doubt very much if we will. You have asked the doctor to come here again, haven't you?"

"Yes, your Grace! As soon as I saw you coming I sent the sexton to the asylum." Then the men went in again into the room which had been the scene of the mysterious crime. The wind rattled the open window and blew out its white curtains. It was already dark in the corners of the room, one could see but indistinctly the carvings of the wainscoting. The light backs of the books, or the gold letters on the darker bindings, made spots of brightness in the gloom. The hideous pool of blood in the centre of the floor was still plainly to be seen.

"Judging by the loss of blood, death must have come quickly."

"There was no struggle, evidently, for everything in the room was in perfect order when we entered it."

"There is not even a chair misplaced. His Bible is there on the desk, he may have been preparing for to-day's sermon."

"Yes, that is the case; because see, here are some notes in his handwriting."

The Count and Judge von Kormendy spoke these sentences at intervals as they made their examination of the room. The local magistrate was able to answer one or two simpler questions, but for the most part he could only shrug his shoulders in helplessness. Nothing had been seen or heard that was at all unusual during the night in the rectory. When the old housekeeper was called up she could say nothing more than this.

Indeed, it was almost impossible for the old woman to say anything, her voice choked with sobs at every second word. None of the household force had noticed anything unusual, or could remember anything at all that would throw light on this mystery.

"Well, then, sir, we might just as well sit down and wait for the detective's arrival," said the judge.

"You are waiting for some one besides the doctor?" asked the local magistrate timidly.

"Yes, His Grace telegraphed to Budapest," answered the district judge, looking at his watch. "And if the train is on time, the man we are waiting for ought to be here in an hour. You sent the carriage to the station, didn't you? Is the driver reliable?"

"Yes, sir, he is a dependable man," said the old housekeeper.

Dr. Orszay entered the room just then and the Count introduced him to the district judge, who was still a stranger to him.

"I fear, Count, that our eyes will serve but little in discovering the truth of this mystery," said the doctor.

The nobleman nodded. "I agree with you," he replied. "And I have sent for sharper eyes than either yours or mine."

The doctor looked his question, and the Count continued: "When the news came to me I telegraphed to Pest for a police detective, telling them that the case was peculiar and urgent. I received an answer as I stopped at the station on my way here. This is it: 'Detective Joseph Muller from Vienna in Budapest by chance. Have sent him to take your case.'"

"Muller?" exclaimed Dr. Orszay. "Can it be the celebrated Muller, the most famous detective of the Austrian police? That would indeed be a blessing."

"I hope and believe that it is," said the Count gravely. "I have heard of this man and we need such a one here that we may find the source of these many misfortunes which have overwhelmed our peaceful village for two years past. It is indeed a stroke of good luck that has led a man of such gifts into our neighbourhood at a time when he is so greatly needed. I believe personally that it is the same person or persons who have been the perpetrators of all these outrages and I intend once for all to put a stop to it, let it cost what it may."

"If any one can discover the truth it will be Muller," said the district judge. "It was I who told the Count how fortunate we were that this man, who is known to the police throughout Austria and far beyond the borders of our kingdom, should have chanced to be in Budapest and free to come to us when we called. You and I" — he turned with a smile to the local magistrate — "you and I can get away with the usual cases of local brutality hereabouts. But the cunning that is at the bottom of these crimes is one too many for us."

The men had taken their places around the great dining-table. The old housekeeper had crept out again, her terror making her forget her usual hospitality. And indeed it would not have occurred to the guests to ask or even to wish for any refreshment. The maid brought a lamp, which sent its weak rays scarcely beyond the edges of the big table. The four men sat in silence for some time.

"I suppose it would be useless to ask who has been coming and going from the rectory the last few days?" began the Count.

"Oh, yes, indeed, sir," said the district judge with a sigh. "For if this murderer is the same who committed the other crimes he must live here in or near the village, and therefore must be known to all and not likely to excite suspicion."

"I beg your pardon, sir," put in the doctor. "There must be at least two of them. One man alone could not have carried off the farm hand who was killed to the swamp where his body was found. Nor could one man alone have taken away the bloody body of the pastor. Our venerable friend was a man of size and weight, as you know, and one man alone could not have dragged his body from he room without leaving an easily seen trail."

The judge blushed, but he nodded in affirmation to the doctor's words. This thought had not occurred to him before. In fact, the judge was more notable for his good will and his love of justice rather than for his keen intelligence. He was as well aware of this as was any one else, and he was heartily glad that the Count had sent to the capital for reinforcements.

Some time more passed in deep silence. Each of the men was occupied with his own thoughts. A sigh broke the silence now and then, and a slight movement when one or the other drew out his watch or raised his head to look at the door. Finally, the sound of a carriage outside was heard. The men sprang up.

The driver's voice was heard, then steps which ascended the stairs lowly and lightly, audible only because the stillness was so great.

The door opened and a small, slight, smooth-shaven man with a gentle face and keen grey eyes stood on the threshold. "I am Joseph Muller," he said with a low, soft voice.

The four men in the room looked at him in astonishment.

"This simple-looking individual is the man that every one is afraid of?" thought the Count, as he walked forward and held out his hand to the stranger.

"I sent for you, Mr. Muller," said the magnate, conscious of his stately size and appearance, as well as of his importance in the presence of a personage who so little looked what his great fame might have led one to expect.

"Then you are Count — — ?" answered Muller gently. "I was in Budapest, having just finished a difficult case which took me there. They told me that a mysterious crime had happened in your neighbourhood, and sent me here to take charge of it. You will pardon any ignorance I may show as a stranger to this locality. I will do my best and it may be possible that I can help you."

The Count introduced the other gentlemen in order and they sat down again at the table.

"And now what is it you want me for, Count?" asked Muller.

"There was a murder committed in this house," answered the Count.

"When?"

"Last night."

"Who is the victim?"

"Our pastor."

"How was he killed?"

"We do not know."

"You are not a physician, then?" asked Muller, turning to Orszay.

"Yes, I am," answered the latter.

"Well?"

"The body is missing," said Orszay, somewhat sharply.

"Missing?" Muller became greatly interested. "Will you please lead me to the scene of the crime?" he said, rising from his chair.

The others led him into the next room, the magistrate going ahead with a lamp. The judge called for more lights and the group stood around the pool of blood on the floor of the study. Muller's arms were crossed on his breast as he stood looking down at the hideous spot. There was no terror in his eyes, as in those of the others, but only a keen attention and a lively interest.

"Who has been in this room since the discovery?" he asked.

The doctor replied that only the servants of the immediate household, the notary, the magistrate, and himself, then later the Count and the district judge entered the room.

"You are quite certain that no one else has been in here?"

"No, no one else."

"Will you kindly send for the three servants?" The magistrate left the room.

"Who else lives in the house?"

"The sexton and the dairymaid."

"And no one else has left the house to-day or has entered it?"

"No one. The main door has been watched all day by a gendarme."

"Is there but one door out of this room?"

"No, there is a small door beside that book-case."

"Where does it lead to?"

"It leads to a passageway at the end of which there is a stair down into the vestry."

Muller gave an exclamation of surprise.

"The vestry as well as the church have neither of them been opened on the side toward the street."

"The church or the vestry, you mean," corrected Muller. "How many doors have they on the street side?"

"One each."

"The locks on these doors were in good condition?"

"Yes, they were untouched."

"Was there anything stolen from the church?"

"No, nothing that we could see."

"Was the pastor rich?"

"No, he was almost a poor man, for he gave away all that he had."

"But you were his patron, Count."

"I was his friend. He was the confidential adviser of myself and family."

"This would mean rich presents now and then, would it not?"

"No, that is not the case. Our venerable pastor would take nothing for himself. He would accept no presents but gifts of money for his poor."

"Then you do not believe this to have been a murder for the sake of robbery?"

"No. There was nothing disturbed in any part of the house, no drawers or cupboards broken open at all."

Muller smiled. "I have heard it said that your romantic Hungarian bandits will often be satisfied with the small booty they may find in the pocket or on the person of their victim."

"You are right, Mr. Muller. But that is only when they can find nothing else."

"Or perhaps if it is a case of revenge.

"It cannot be revenge in this case!"

"The pastor was greatly loved?"

"He was loved and revered."

"By every one?"

"By every one!" the four men answered at once.

Muller was still a while. His eyes were veiled and his face thoughtful. Finally he raised his head. "There has been nothing moved or changed in this room?"

"No — neither here nor anywhere else in the house or the church," answered the local magistrate.

"That is good. Now I would like to question the servants."

Muller had already started for the door, then he turned back into the room and pointing toward the second door he asked: "Is that door locked?"

"Yes," answered the Count. "I found it locked when I examined it myself a short time ago."

"It was locked on the inside?"

"Yes, locked on the inside."

"Very well. Then we have nothing more to do here for the time being. Let us go back into the dining-room."

The men returned to the dining-room, Muller last, for he stopped to lock the door of the study and put the key in his pocket. Then he began his examination of the servants.

The old housekeeper, who, as usual, was the first to rise in the household, had also, as usual, rung the bell to waken the other servants. Then when Liska came downstairs she had sent her up to the pastor's room. His bedroom was to the right of the dining-room. Liska had, as usual, knocked on the door exactly at seven o'clock and continued knocking for some few minutes without receiving any answer. Slightly alarmed, the girl had gone back and told the housekeeper that the pastor did not answer.

Then the old woman asked the coachman to go up and see if anything was the matter with the reverend gentleman. The man returned in a few moments, pale and trembling in every limb and apparently struck dumb by fright. He motioned the women to follow him, and all three crept up the stairs. The coachman led them first to the pastor's bed, which was untouched, and then to the pool of blood in his study. The sight of the latter frightened the servants so much that they did not notice at first that there was no sign of the pastor himself, whom they now knew must have been murdered. When they finally came to themselves sufficiently to take some action, the man hurried off to call the magistrate, and Liska ran to the asylum to fetch the old doctor; the pastor's intimate friend. The aged housekeeper, trembling in fear, crept back to her own room and sat there waiting the return of the others.

This was the story of the early morning as told by the three servants, who had already given their report in much the same words to the Count on his arrival and also to the magistrate. There was no reason to doubt the words of either the old housekeeper or of Janos, the coachman, who had served for more than twenty years in the rectory and whose fidelity was known. The girl Liska was scarcely eighteen, and her round childish face and big eyes dimmed with tears, corroborated her story. When they had told Muller all they knew, the detective sat stroking, his chin, and looking thoughtfully at the floor. Then he raised his head and said, in a tone of calm friendliness: "Well, good friends, this will do for tonight. Now, if you will kindly give me a bite to eat and a glass of some light wine, I'd be very thankful. I have had no food since early this morning."

The housekeeper and the maid disappeared, and Janos went to the stable to harness the Count's trap.

The magnate turned to the detective. "I thank you once more that you have come to us. I appreciate it greatly that a stranger to our part of the country, like yourself, should give his time and strength to this problem of our obscure little village."

"There is nothing else calling me, sir," answered Muller. "And the Budapest police will explain to headquarters at Vienna if I do not return at once."

"Do you understand our tongue sufficiently to deal with these people here?"

"Oh, yes; there will be no difficulty about that. I have hunted criminals in Hungary before. And a case of this kind does not usually call for disguises in which any accent would betray one."

"It is a strange profession," said the doctor.

"One gets used to it — like everything else," answered Muller, with a gentle smile. "And now I have to thank you gentlemen for your confidence in me."

"Which I know you will justify," said the Count.

Muller shrugged his shoulders: "I haven't felt anything yet — but it will come — there's something in the air."

The Count smiled at his manner of expressing himself, but all four of the men had already begun to feel sympathy and respect for this quiet-mannered little person whose words were so few and whose voice was so gentle. Something in his grey eyes and in the quiet determination of his manner made them realise that he had won his fame honestly. With the enthusiasm of his race the Hungarian Count pressed the detective's hand in a warm grasp as he said: "I know that we can trust in you. You will avenge the death of my old friend and of those others who were killed here. The doctor and the magistrate will tell you about them to-morrow. We two will go home now. Telegraph us as soon as anything has happened. Every one in the village will be ready to help you and of course you can call on me for funds. Here is something to begin on." With these words the Count laid a silk purse full of gold pieces on the table. One more pressure of the hand and he was gone. The other men also left the room, following the Count's lead in a cordial farewell of the detective. They also shared the nobleman's feeling that now indeed, with this man to help them, could the cloud of horror that had hung over the village for two years, and had culminated in the present catastrophe, be lifted.

The excitement of the Count's departure had died away and the steps of the other men on their way to the village had faded in the distance. There was nothing now to be heard but the rustling of the leaves and the creaking of the boughs as the trees bent before the onrush of the wind. Muller stood alone, with folded arms, in the middle of the large room, letting his sharp eyes wander about the circle of light thrown by the lamps. He was glad to be alone — for only when he was alone could his brain do its best work. He took up one of the lamps and opened the door to the room in which, as far as could be known, the murder had been committed. He walked in carefully and, setting the lamp on the desk, examined the articles lying about on it. There was nothing of importance to be found there. An open Bible and a sheet of paper with notes for the day's sermon lay on top of the desk. In the drawers, none of which were locked, were official papers, books, manuscripts of former sermons, and a few unimportant personal notes.

The flame of the lamp flickered in the breeze that came from the open window. But Muller did not close the casement. He wanted to leave everything just as he had found it until daylight. When he saw that it was impossible to leave the lamp there he took it up again and left the room.

"What is the use of being impatient?" he said to himself. "If I move about in this poor light I will be sure to ruin some possible clue. For there must be some clue left here. It is impossible for even the most practiced criminal not to leave some trace of his presence."

The detective returned to the dining-room, locking the study door carefully behind him. The maid and the coachman returned, bringing in an abundant supper, and Muller sat down to do justice to the many good things on the tray. When the maid returned to take away the dishes she inquired whether she should put the guest chamber in order for the detective. He told her not to go to any trouble for his sake, that he would sleep in the bed in the neighbouring room.

"You going to sleep in there?" said the girl, horrified.

"Yes, my child, and I think I will sleep well

to-night. I feel very tired." Liska carried the things out, shaking her head in surprise at this thin little man who did not seem to know what it was to be afraid. Half an hour later the rectory was in darkness. Before he retired, Muller had made a careful examination of the pastor's bedroom. Nothing was disturbed anywhere, and it was evident that the priest had not made any preparations for the night, but was still at work at his desk in the study when death overtook him. When he came to this conclusion, the detective went to bed and soon fell asleep.

In his little hut near the asylum gates, shepherd Janci slept as sound as usual. But he was dreaming and he spoke in his sleep. There was no one to hear him, for his faithful Margit was snoring loudly. Snatches of sentences and broken words came from Janci's lips: "The hand — the big hand — I see it — at his throat — the face — the yellow face — it laughs — "

Next morning the children on their way to school crept past the rectory with wide eyes and open mouths. And the grown people spoke in lower tones when their work led them past the handsome old house. It had once been their pride, but now it was a place of horror to them. The old housekeeper had succumbed to her fright and was very ill. Liska went about her work silently, and the farm servants walked more heavily and chattered less than they had before. The hump-backed sexton, who had not been allowed to enter the church and therefore had nothing to do, made an early start for the inn, where he spent most of the day telling what little he knew to the many who made an excuse to follow him there.

The only calm and undisturbed person in the rectory household was Muller. He had made a thorough examination of the entire scene of the murder, but had not found anything at all. Of one thing alone was he certain: the murderer had come through the hidden passageway from the church. There were two reasons to believe this, one of which might possibly not be sufficient, but the other was conclusive.

The heavy armchair before the desk, the chair on which the pastor was presumably sitting when the murderer entered, was half turned around, turned in just such a way as it would have been had the man who was sitting there suddenly sprung up in excitement or surprise. The chair was pushed back a step from the desk and turned towards the entrance to the passageway. Those who had been in the room during the day had reported that they had not touched any one of the articles of furniture, therefore the position of the chair was the same that had been given it by the man who had sat in it, by the murdered pastor himself.

Of course there was always the possibility that some one had moved the chair without realising it. This clue, therefore, could not be looked upon as an absolutely certain one had it stood alone. But there was other evidence far more important. The great pool of blood was just half-way between the door of the passage and the armchair. It was here, therefore, that the attack had taken place. The pastor could not have turned in this direction in the hope of flight, for there was nothing here to give him shelter, no weapon that he could grasp, not even a cane. He must have turned in this direction to meet and greet the invader who had entered his room in this unusual manner. Turned to meet him as a brave man would, with no other weapon than the sacredness of his calling and his age.

But this had not been enough to protect the venerable priest. The murderer must have made his thrust at once and his victim had sunk down dying on the floor of the room in which he had spent so many hours of quiet study, in which he had brought comfort and given advice to so many anxious hearts; for dying he must have been — it would be impossible for a man to lose so much blood and live.

"The struggle," thought the detective, "but was there a struggle?" He looked about the room again, but could see nothing that showed disorder anywhere in its immaculate neatness. No, there could have been no struggle. It must have been a quick knife thrust and death at once. "Not a shot?" No, a shot would have been heard by the night watchman walking the streets near the church. The night was quiet, the window open. Some one in the village would have heard the noise of a shot. And it was not likely that the old housekeeper who slept in the room immediately below, slept the light sleep of the aged would have failed to have heard the firing of a pistol.

Muller took a chair and sat down directly in front of the pool of blood, looking at it carefully. Suddenly he bowed his head deeper. He had caught sight of a fine thread of the red fluid which had been drawn out for about a foot or two in the direction towards the door to the dining-room. What did that mean? Did it mean that the murderer went out through that door, dragging something after him that made this delicate line? Muller bent down still deeper. The sun shone brightly on the floor, sending its clear rays obliquely through the window. The sharp eyes which now covered every inch of the yellow-painted floor discovered something else. They discovered that this red thread curved slightly and had a continuation in a fine scratch in the paint of the floor. Muller followed up this scratch and it led him over towards the window and then back again in wide curves, then out again under the desk and finally, growing weaker and weaker, it came back to the neighbourhood of the pool of blood, but on the opposite side of it. Muller got down on his hands and knees to follow up the scratch. He did not notice the discomfort of his position, his eyes shone in excitement and a deep flush glowed in his cheeks. Also, he began to whistle softly.

Joseph Muller, the bloodhound of the Austrian police, had found a clue, a clue that soon would bring him to the trail he was seeking. He did not know yet what he could do with his clue. But this much he knew; sooner or later this scratch in the floor would lead him to the murderer. The trail might be long and devious; but he would follow it and at its end would be success. He knew that this scratch had been made after the murder was committed; this was proved by the blood that marked its beginning. And it could not have been made by any of those who entered the room during the day because by that time the blood had dried. This strange streak in the floor, with its weird curves and spirals, could have been made only by the murderer. But how? With what instrument? There was the riddle which must be solved.

And now Muller, making another careful examination of the floor, found something else. It was something that might be utterly unimportant or might be of great value. It was a tiny bit of hardened lacquer which he found on the floor beside one of the legs of the desk. It was rounded out, with sharp edges, and coloured grey with a tiny zigzag of yellow on its surface. Muller lifted it carefully and looked at it keenly. This tiny bit of lacquer had evidently been knocked off from some convex object, but it was impossible to tell at the moment just what sort of an object it might have been. There are so many different things which are customarily covered with lacquer. However, further examination brought him down to a narrower range of subjects. For on the inside of the lacquer he found a shred of reddish wood fibre. It must have been a wooden object, therefore, from which the lacquer came, and the wood had been of reddish tinge.

Muller pondered the matter for a little while longer. Then he placed his discovery carefully in the pastor's emptied tobacco-box, and dropped the box in his own pocket. He closed the window and the door to the dining-room, lit a lamp, and entered the passageway leading to the vestry. It was a short passageway, scarcely more than a dozen paces long.

The walls were whitewashed, the floor tiled and the entire passage shone in neatness. Muller held the light of his lamp to every inch of it, but there was nothing to show that the criminal had gone through here with the body of his victim.

"The criminal" — Muller still thought of only one. His long experience had taught him that the most intricate crimes were usually committed by one man only. The strength necessary for such a crime as this did not deceive him either. He knew that in extraordinary moments extraordinary strength will come to the one who needs it.

He now passed down the steps leading into the vestry. There was no trace of any kind here either. The door into the vestry was not locked. It was seldom locked, they had told him, for the vestry itself was closed by a huge carved portal with a heavy ornamented iron lock that could be opened only with the greatest noise and trouble. This door was locked and closed as it had been since yesterday morning. Everything in the vestry was in perfect order; the priest's garments and the censers all in their places. Muller assured himself of this before he left the little room. He then opened the glass door that led down by a few steps into the church.

It was a beautiful old church, and it was a rich church also. It was built in the older Gothic style, and its heavy, broad-arched walls, its massive columns would have made it look cold and bare had not handsome tapestries, the gift of the lady of the manor, covered the walls. Fine old pictures hung here and there above the altars, and handsome stained glass windows broke the light that fell into the high vaulted interior. There were three great altars in the church, all of them richly decorated. The main altar stood isolated in the choir. In the open space behind it was the entrance to the crypt, now veiled in a mysterious twilight. Heavy silver candlesticks, three on a side, stood on the altar. The pale gold of the tabernacle door gleamed between them.

Muller walked through the silent church, in which even his light steps resounded uncannily. He looked into each of the pews, into the confessionals, he walked around all the columns, he climbed up into the pulpit, he did everything that the others had done before him yesterday. And as with them, he found nothing that would indicate that the murderer had spent any time in the church. Finally he turned back once more to the main altar on his way out. But he did not leave the church as he intended. His last look at the altar had showed him something that attracted his attention and he walked up the three steps to examine it more closely.

What he had seen was something unusual about one of the silver candlesticks. These candlesticks had three feet, and five of them were placed in such a way that the two front feet were turned toward the spectator. But on the end candlestick nearest Muller the single foot projected out to the front of the altar. This candlestick therefore had been set down hastily, not placed carefully in the order of things as were the others.

And not only this. The heavy wax candle which was in the candlestick was burned down about a finger's breadth more than the others, for these were all exactly of a height. Muller bent still nearer to the candlestick, but he saw that the dim light in the church was not sufficient. He went to one of the smaller side altars, took a candle from there, lit it with one of the matches that he found in his own pocket and returned with the burning candle to the main altar. The steps leading up to this altar were covered by a large rug with a white ground and a pattern of flowers. Looking carefully at it the detective saw a tiny brown spot, the mark of a burn, upon one of the white surfaces. Beside it lay a half used match.

Walking around this carefully, Muller approached the candlestick that interested him and holding up his light he examined every inch of its surface. He found what he was looking for. There were dark red spots between the rough edges of the silver ornamentation.

"Then the body is somewhere around here," thought the detective and came down from the steps, still holding the burning candle.

He walked slowly to the back of the altar. There was a little table there such as held the sacred dishes for the communion service, and the little carpet-covered steps which the sexton put out for the pastor when he took the monstrance from the high-built tabernacle. That was all that was to be seen in the dark corner behind the altar. Holding his candle close to the floor Muller discovered an iron ring fastened to one of the big stone flags. This must be the entrance to the crypt.

Muller tried to raise the flag and was astonished to find how easily it came up. It was a square of reddish marble, the same with which the entire floor of the church was tiled. This flag was very thin and could easily be raised and placed back against the wall. Muller took up his candle, too greatly excited to stop to get a stick for it. He felt assured that now he would soon be able to solve at least a part of the mystery. He climbed down the steps carefully and found that they led into the crypt as he supposed. They were kept spotlessly clean, as was the entire crypt as far as he could see it by the light of his flickering candle. He was not surprised to discover that the air was perfectly pure here. There must be windows or ventilators somewhere, this he knew from the way his candle behaved.

The ancient vault had a high arched ceiling and heavy massive pillars. It was a subterranean repetition of the church above. There had evidently been a convent attached to this church at one time; for here stood a row of simple wooden coffins all exactly alike, bearing each one upon its lid a roughly painted cross surrounded by a wreath. Thus were buried the monks of days long past.

Muller walked slowly through the rows of coffins looking eagerly to each side. Suddenly he stopped and stood still. His hand did not tremble but his thin face was pale — pale as that face which looked up at him out of one of the coffins. The lid of the coffin stood up against the wall and Muller saw that there were several other empty ones further on, waiting for their silent occupants.

The body in the open coffin before which Muller stood was the body of the man who had been missing since the day previous. He lay there quite peacefully, his hands crossed over his breast, his eyes closed, a line of pain about his lips. In the crossed fingers was a little bunch of dark yellow roses. At the first glance one might almost have thought that loving hands had laid the old pastor in his coffin. But the red stain on the white cloth about his throat, and the bloody disorder of his snow-white hair contrasted sadly with the look of peace on the dead face. Under his head was a white silk cushion, one of the cushions from the altar.

Muller stood looking down for some time at this poor victim of a strange crime, then he turned to go.

He wanted to know one thing more: how the murderer had left the crypt. The flame of his candle told him, for it nearly went out in a gust of wind that came down the opening right above him. This was a window about three or four feet from the floor, protected by rusty iron bars which had been sawed through, leaving the opening free. It was a small window, but it was large enough to allow a man of much greater size than Muller to pass through it. The detective blew out his candle and climbed up onto the window sill. He found himself outside, in a corner of the churchyard. A thicket of heavy bushes grown up over neglected graves completely hid the opening through which he had come. There were thorns on these bushes and also a few scattered roses, dark yellow roses.

Muller walked thoughtfully through the churchyard. The sexton sat huddled in an unhappy heap at the gate. He looked up in alarm as he saw the detective walking towards him. Something in the stranger's face told the little hunchback that he had made a discovery. The sexton sprang up, his lips did not dare utter the question that his eyes asked.

"I have found him," said the detective gravely.

The hunchback sexton staggered, then recovered himself, and hurried away to fetch the magistrate and the doctor.

An hour later the murdered pastor lay in state in the chief apartment of his home, surrounded by burning candles and high-heaped masses of flowers. But he still lay in the simple convent coffin and the little bunch of roses which his murderer had placed between his stiffening fingers had not been touched.

Two days later the pastor was buried. The Count and his family led the train of numerous mourners and among the last was Muller.

A day or two after the funeral the detective sauntered slowly through the main street of the village. He was not in a very good humour, his answer to the greeting of those who passed him was short. The children avoided him, for with the keenness of their kind they recognised the fact that this usually gentle little man was not in possession of his habitual calm temper. One group of boys, playing with a top, did not notice his coming and Muller stopped behind them to look on. Suddenly a sharp whistle was heard and the boys looked up from their play, surprised at seeing the stranger behind them. His eyes were gleaming, and his cheeks were flushed, and a few bars of a merry tune came in a keen whistle from his lips as he watched the spirals made by the spinning top.

Before the boys could stop their play the detective had left the group and hastened onward to the little shop. He left it again in eager haste after having made his purchase, and hurried back to the rectory. The shop-keeper stood in the doorway looking in surprise at this grown man who came to buy a top. And at home in the rectory the old housekeeper listened in equal surprise to the humming noise over her head. She thought at first it might be a bee that had got in somehow. Then she realised that it was not quite the same noise, and having already concluded that it was of no use to be surprised at anything this strange guest might do, she continued reading her scriptures.

Upstairs in the pastor's study, Muller sat in the armchair attentively watching the gyrations of a spinning top. The little toy, started at a certain point, drew a line exactly parallel to the scratch on the floor that had excited his thoughts and absorbed them day and night.

"It was a top — a top" repeated the detective to himself again and again. "I don't see why I didn't think of that right away. Why, of course, nothing else could have drawn such a perfect curve around the room, unhindered by the legs of the desk. Only I don't see how a toy like that could have any connection with this cruel and purposeless murder. Why, only a fool — or a madman — "

Muller sprang up from his chair and again a sharp shrill whistle came from his lips. "A madman! — " he repeated, beating his own forehead. "It could only have been a madman who committed this murder! And the pastor was not the first, there were two other murders here within a comparatively short time. I think I will take advantage of Dr. Orszay's invitation."

Half an hour later Muller and the doctor sat together in a summer-house, from the windows of which one could see the park surrounding the asylum to almost its entire extent. The park was arranged with due regard to its purpose. The eye could sweep through it unhindered. There were no bushes except immediately along the high wall. Otherwise there were beautiful lawns, flower beds and groups of fine old trees with tall trunks.

As would be natural in visiting such a place Muller had induced the doctor to talk about his patients. Dr. Orszay was an excellent talker and possessed the power of painting a personality for his listeners. He was pleased and flattered by the evident interest with which the detective listened to his remarks.

"Then your patients are all quite harmless?" asked Muller thoughtfully, when the doctor came to a pause.

"Yes, all quite harmless. Of course, there is the man who strangely enough considers himself the reincarnation of the famous French murderer, the goldsmith Cardillac, who, as you remember, kept all Paris in a fervour of excitement by his crimes during the reign of Louis XIV. But in spite of his weird mania this man is the most good-natured of any. He has been shut up in his room for several days now. He was a mechanician by trade, living in Budapest, and an unsuccessful invention turned his mind."

"Is he a large, powerful man?" asked Muller.

Dr. Orszay looked a bit surprised. "Why do you ask that? He does happen to be a large man of considerable strength, but in spite of it I have no fear of him. I have an attendant who is invaluable to me, a man of such strength that even the fiercest of them cannot overcome him, and yet with a mind and a personal magnetism which they cannot resist. He can always master our patients mentally and physically — most of them are afraid of him and they know that they must do as he says. There is something in his very glance which has the power to paralyse even healthy nerves, for it shows the strength of will possessed by this man."

"And what is the name of this invaluable attendant?" asked Muller with a strange smile which the doctor took to be slightly ironical.

"Gyuri Kovacz. You are amused at my enthusiasm? But consider my position here. I am an old man and have never been a strong man. At my age I would not have strength enough to force that little woman there — she thinks herself possessed and is quite cranky at times — to go to her own room when she doesn't want to. And do you see that man over there in the blue blouse? He is an excellent gardener but he believes himself to be Napoleon, and when he has his acute attacks I would be helpless to control him were it not for Gyuri."

"And you are not afraid of Cardillac?" interrupted Muller.

"Not in the least. He is as good-natured as a child and as confiding. I can let him walk around here as much as he likes. If it were not for the absurd nonsense that he talks when he has one of his attacks, and which frightens those who do not understand him, I could let him go free altogether."

"Then you never let him leave the asylum grounds?

"Oh, yes. I take him out with me very frequently. He is a man of considerable education and a very clever talker. It is quite a pleasure to be with him. That was the opinion of my poor friend also, my poor murdered friend."

"The pastor?"

"The pastor. He often invited Cardillac to come to the rectory with me."

"Indeed. Then Cardillac knew the inside of the rectory?"

"Yes. The pastor used to lend him books and let him choose them himself from the library shelves. The people in the village are very kind to my poor patients here. I have long since had the habit of taking some of the quieter ones with me down into the village and letting the people become acquainted with them. It is good for both parties. It gives the patients some little diversion, and it takes away the worst of the senseless fear these peasants had at first of the asylum and its inmates. Cardillac in particular is always welcome when he comes, for he brings the children all sorts of toys that he makes in his cell."

The detective had listened attentively and once his eyes flashed and his lips shut tight as if to keep in the betraying whistle. Then he asked calmly: "But the patients are only allowed to go out when you accompany them, I suppose?"

"Oh, no; the attendants take them out sometimes. I prefer, however, to let them go only with

Gyuri, for I can depend upon him more than upon any of the others."

"Then he and Cardillac have been out together occasionally?"

"Oh, yes, quite frequently. But — pardon me — this is almost like a cross-examination."

"I beg your pardon, doctor, it's a bad habit of mine. One gets so accustomed to it in my profession."

"What is it you want?" asked Doctor Orszay, turning to a fine-looking young man of superb build, who entered just then and stood by the door.

"I just wanted to announce, sir, that No. 302 is quiet again!

"302 is Cardillac himself, Mr. Muller, or to give him his right name, Lajos Varna," explained the doctor turning to his guest. "He is the 302nd patient who has been received here in these twenty years. Then Cardillac is quiet again?" he asked, looking up at the young giant. "I am glad of that. You can announce our visit to him. This gentleman wants to inspect the asylum."

Muller realised that this was the attendant Gyuri, and he looked at him attentively. He was soon clear in his own mind that this remarkably handsome man did not please him, in fact awoke in him a feeling of repulsion. The attendant's quiet, almost cat-like movements were in strange contrast to the massivity of his superb frame, and his large round eyes, shaped for open, honest glances, were shifty and cunning. They seemed to be asking "Are you trying to discover anything about me?" coupled with a threat. "For your own sake you had better not do it."

When the young man had left the room Muller rose hastily and walked up and down several times. His face was flushed and his lips tight set. Suddenly he exclaimed: "I do not like this Gyuri."

Dr. Orszay looked up astonished. "There are many others who do not like him — most of his fellow-warders for instance, and all of the patients. I think there must be something in the contrast of such quiet movements with such a big body that gets on people's nerves. But consider, Mr. Muller, that the man's work would naturally make him a little different from other people. I have known Gyuri for five years as a faithful and unassuming servant, always willing and ready for any duty, however difficult or dangerous. He has but one fault — if I may call it such — that is that he has a mistress who is known to be mercenary and hard-hearted. She lives in a neighbouring village."

"For five years, you say? And how long has Cardillac been here?"

"Cardillac? He has been here for almost three years."

"For almost three years, and is it not almost

three years — " Muller interrupted himself. "Are we quite alone? Is no one listening?" The doctor nodded, greatly surprised, and the detective continued almost in a whisper, "and it is just about three years now that there have been committed, at intervals, three terrible crimes notable from the cleverness with which they were carried out, and from the utter impossibility, apparently, of discovering the perpetrator."

Orszay sprang up. His face flushed and then grew livid, and he put his hand to his forehead. Then he forced a smile and said in a voice that trembled in spite of himself: "Mr. Muller, your imagination is wonderful. And which of these two do you think it is that has committed these crimes — the perpetrator of which you have come here to find?"

"I will tell you that later. I must speak to No. 302 first, and I must speak to him in the presence of yourself and Gyuri."

The detective's deep gravity was contagious. Dr. Orszay had sufficiently controlled himself to remember what he had heard in former days, and just now recently from the district judge about this man's marvelous deeds. He realised that when Muller said a thing, no matter how extravagant it might sound, it was worth taking seriously. This realisation brought great uneasiness and grief to the doctor's heart, for he had grown fond of both of the men on whom terrible suspicion was cast by such an authority.

Muller himself was uneasy, but the gloom that had hung over him for the past day or two had vanished. The impenetrable darkness that had surrounded the mystery of the pastor's murder had gotten on his nerves. He was not accustomed to work so long over a problem without getting some light on it. But now, since the chance watching of the spinning top in the street had given him his first inkling of the trail, he was following it up to a clear issue. The eagerness, the blissful vibrating of every nerve that he always felt at this stage of the game, was on him again. He knew that from now on what was still to be done would be easy. Hitherto his mind had been made up on one point; that one man alone was concerned in the crime. Now he understood the possibility that there might have been two, the harmless mechanician who fancied himself a dangerous murderer, and the handsome young giant with the evil eyes.

The two men stood looking at each other in a silence that was almost hostile. Had this stranger come to disturb the peace of the refuge for the unfortunate and to prove that Dr. Orszay, the friend of all the village, had unwittingly been giving shelter to such criminals?

"Shall we go now?" asked the detective finally.

"If you wish it, sir," answered the doctor in a tone that was decidedly cool.

Muller held out his hand. "Don't let us be foolish, doctor. If you should find yourself terribly deceived, and I should have been the means of proving it, promise me that you will not be angry with me."

Orszay pressed the offered hand with a deep sigh. He realised the other's position and knew it was his duty to give him every possible assistance. "What is there for me to do now?" he asked sadly.

"You must see that all the patients are shut up in their cells so that the other attendants are at our disposal if we need them. Varna's room has barred windows, I suppose?"

"Yes."

"And I suppose also that it has but one door. I believe you told me that your asylum was built on the cell system."

"Yes, there is but one door to the room."

"Let the four other attendants stand outside this door. Gyuri will be inside with us. Tell the men outside that they are to seize and hold whomever I shall designate to them. I will call them in by a whistle. You can trust your people?"

"Yes, I think I can."

"Well, I have my revolver," said Muller calmly, "and now we can go."

They left the room together, and found Gyuri

waiting for them a little further along the corridor. "Aren't you well, sir?" the attendant asked the doctor, with an anxious note in his voice.

The man's anxiety was not feigned. He was really a faithful servant in his devotion to the old doctor, although Muller had not misjudged him when he decided that this young giant was capable of anything. Good and evil often lie so close together in the human heart.

The doctor's emotion prevented him from speaking, and the detective answered in his place. "It is a sudden indisposition," he said. "Lead me to No. 302, who is waiting for us, I suppose. The doctor wants to lie down a moment in his own room."

Gyuri glanced distrustfully at this man whom he had met for the first time to-day, but who was no stranger to him — for he had already learned the identity of the guest in the rectory. Then he turned his eyes on his master. The latter nodded and said: "Take the gentleman to Varna's room. I will follow shortly."

The cell to which they went was the first one at the head of the staircase. "Extremely convenient," thought Muller to himself. It was a large room, comfortably furnished and filled now with the red glow of the setting sun. A turning-lathe stood by the window and an elderly man was at work at it. Gyuri called to him and he turned and rose when he saw a stranger.

Lajos Varna was a tall, loose-jointed man with sallow skin and tired eyes. He gave only a hasty glance at his visitor, then looked at Gyuri. The expression in his eyes as he turned them on those of the warder was like the look in the eyes of a well-trained dog when it watches its master's face. Gyuri's brows were drawn close together and his mouth set tight to a narrow line. His eyes fairly bored themselves into the patient's eyes with an expression like that of a hypnotiser.

Muller knew now what he wanted to know. This young man understood how to bend the will of others, even the will of a sick mind, to his own desires. The little silent scene he had watched had lasted just the length of time it had taken the detective to walk through the room and hold out his hand to the patient.

"I don't want to disturb you, Mr. Varna," he said in a friendly tone, with a motion towards the bench from which the mechanician had just arisen. Varna sat down again, obedient as a child. He was not always so apparently, for Muller saw a red mark over the fingers of one hand that was evidently the mark of a blow. Gyuri was not very choice in the methods by which he controlled the patients confided to his care.

"May I sit down also?" asked Muller.

Varna pushed forward a chair. His movements were like those of an automaton.

"And now tell me how you like it here?" began the detective. Varna answered with a low soft voice, "Oh, I like it very much, sir." As he spoke he looked up at Gyuri, whose eyes still bore their commanding expression.

"They treat you kindly here?"

"Oh, yes."

"The doctor is very good to you?"

"Ah, the doctor is so good!" Varna's dull eyes brightened.

"And the others are good to you also?"

"Oh, yes." The momentary gleam in the sad had vanished again.

"Where did you get this red scar?"

The patient became uneasy, he moved anxiously on his chair and looked up at Gyuri. It was evident that he realised there would be more red marks if he told the truth to this stranger.

Muller did not insist upon an answer. "You are uneasy and nervous sometimes, aren't you?"

"Yes, sir, I have been — nervous — lately."

"And they don't let you go out at such times?"

"Why, I — no, I may not go out at such times."

"But the doctor takes you with him sometimes — the doctor or Gyuri?" asked the detective.

"Yes."

"I haven't had him out with me for weeks," interrupted the attendant. He seemed particularly anxious to have the "for weeks" clearly heard by this inconvenient questioner.

Muller dropped this subject and took up another. "They tell me you are very fond of children, and I can see that you are making toys for them here."

"Yes, I love children, and I am so glad they are not afraid of me." These words were spoken with more warmth and greater interest than anything the man had yet said.

"And they tell me that you take gifts with you for the children every time you go down to the village. This is pretty work here, and it must be a pleasant diversion for you." Muller had taken up a dainty little spinning-wheel which was almost completed. "Isn't it made from the wood of a red yew tree?"

"Yes, the doctor gave me a whole tree that had been cut down in the park."

"And that gave you wood for a long time?"

"Yes, indeed; I have been making toys from it for months." Varna had become quite eager and interested as he handed his visitor a number of pretty trifles. The two had risen from their chairs and were leaning over the wide window seat which served as a store-house for the wares turned out by the busy workman. They were toys, mostly, all sorts of little pots and plates, dolls' furniture, balls of various sizes, miniature bowling pins, and tops. Muller took up one of the latter.

"How very clever you are, and how industrious," he exclaimed, sitting down again and turning the top in his hands. It was covered with gray varnish with tiny little yellow stripes painted on it. Towards the lower point a little bit of the varnish had been broken off and the reddish wood underneath was visible. The top was much better constructed than the cheap toys sold in the village. It was hollow and contained in its interior a mechanism started by a pressure on the upper end. Once set in motion the little top spun about the room for some time.

"Oh, isn't that pretty! Is this mechanism your own invention?" asked Muller smiling. Gyuri watched the top with drawn brows and murmured something about "childish foolishness."

"Yes, it is my own invention," said the patient, flattered. He started out on an absolutely technical explanation of the mechanism of tops in general and of his own in particular, an explanation so lucid and so well put that no one would have believed the man who was speaking was not in possession of the full powers of his mind.

Muller listened very attentively with un-feigned interest.

"But you have made more important inventions than this, haven't you?" he asked when the other stopped talking. Varna's eyes flashed and his voice dropped to a tone of mystery as he answered: "Yes indeed I have. But I did not have time to finish them. For I had become some one else."

"Some one else?"

"Cardillac," whispered Varna, whose mania was now getting the best of him again.

"Cardillac? You mean the notorious gold-smith who lived in Paris 200 years ago? Why, he's dead."

Varna's pale lips curled in a superior smile. "Oh, yes — that's what people think, but it's a mistake. He is still alive — I am — I have — although of course there isn't much opportunity here — "

Gyuri cleared his throat with a rasping noise.

"What were you saying, friend Cardillac?" asked Muller with a great show of interest.

"I have done things here that nobody has found out. It gives me great pleasure to see the authorities so helpless over the riddles I have given them to solve. Oh, indeed, sir, you would never imagine how stupid they are here."

"In other words, friend Cardillac, you are too clever for the authorities here?

"Yes, that's it," said the insane man greatly flattered. He raised his head proudly and smiled down at his guest. At this moment the doctor came into the room and Gyuri walked forward to the group at the window.

"You are making him nervous, sir," he said to Muller in a tone that was almost harsh.

"You can leave that to me," answered the detective calmly. "And you will please place yourself behind Mr. Varna's chair, not behind mine. It is your eyes that are making him uneasy."

The attendant was alarmed and lost control of himself for a moment. "Sir!" he exclaimed in an outburst.

"My name is Muller, in case you do not know it already, Joseph Muller, detective. Gyuri Kovacz, you will do what I tell you to! I am master here just now. Is it not so, doctor?"

"Yes, it is so," said the doctor.

"What does this mean?" murmured Gyuri, turning pale.

"It means that the best thing for you to do is to stand up against that wall and fold your arms on your breast," said Muller firmly. He took a revolver from his pocket and laid it beside him on the turning-lathe. The young giant, cowed by the sight of the weapon, obeyed the commands of this little man whom he could have easily crushed with a single blow.

Dr. Orszay sank down on the chair beside the door. Muller, now completely master of the situation, turned to the insane man who stood looking at him in a surprise which was mingled with admiration.

"And now, my dear Cardillac, you must tell us of your great deeds here," said the detective in a friendly tone.

The unfortunate man bent over him with shining eyes and whispered: "But you'll shoot him first, won't you?"

"Why should I shoot him?"

"Because he won't let me say a word without beating me. He is so cruel. He sticks pins into me if I don't do what he wants."

"Why didn't you tell the doctor?"

"Gyuri would have treated me worse than ever then. I am a coward, sir, I'm so afraid of pain and he knew that — he knew that I was afraid of being hurt and that I'd always do what he asked of me. And because I don't like to be hurt myself I always finished them off quickly."

"Finished who?"

"Why, there was Red Betty, he wanted her money."

"Who wanted it?"

"Gyuri."

The man at the wall moved when he heard this terrible accusation. But the detective took up his revolver again. "Be quiet there!" he called, with a look such as he might have thrown at an angry dog. Gyuri stood quiet again but his eyes shot flames and great drops stood out on his forehead.

"Now go on, friend Cardillac," continued the detective. "We were talking about Red Betty."

"I strangled her. She did not even know she was dying. She was such a weak old woman, it really couldn't have hurt her."

"No, certainly not," said Muller soothingly, for he saw that the thought that his victim might have suffered was beginning to make the madman uneasy. "You needn't worry about that. Old Betty died a quiet death. But tell me, how did Gyuri know that she had money?"

"The whole village knew it. She laid cards for people and earned a lot of money that way. She was very stingy and saved every bit. Somebody saw her counting out her money once, she had it in a big stocking under her bed. People in the village talked about it. That's how Gyuri heard of it."

"And so he commanded you to kill Betty and steal her money?"

"Yes. He knew that I loved to give them riddles to guess, just as I did in Paris so long ago."

"Oh, yes, you're Cardillac, aren't you? And now tell us about the smith's swineherd."

"You mean Janos? Oh, he was a stupid lout," answered Varna scornfully.

"He had cast an eye on the beautiful Julcsi, Gyuri's mistress, so of course I had to kill him."

"Did you do that alone?"

"No, Gyuri helped me."

"Why did you cut the bridge supports?"

"Because I enjoy giving people riddles, as I told you. But Gyuri forbade me to kill people uselessly. I liked the chance of getting out though. The doctor's so good to me and the others too. Gyuri is good to me when I have done what he wanted. But you see, Mr. Muller, I am like a prisoner here and that makes me angry. I made Gyuri let me out nights sometimes."

"You mean he let you out alone, all alone?"

"Yes, of course, for I threatened to tell the doctor everything if he didn't."

"You wouldn't have dared do that."

"No, that's true," smiled Varna slyly. "But Gyuri was afraid I might do it, for he isn't always strong enough to frighten me with his eyes. Those were the hours when I could make him afraid — I liked those hours — "

"What did you do when you were out alone at night?"

"I just walked about. I set fire to a tree in the woods once, then the rain came and put it out. Once I killed a dog and another time I cut through the bridge supports. That took me several hours to do and made me very tired. But it was such fun to know that people would be worrying and fussing about who did it."

Varna rubbed his hands gleefully. He did not look the least bit malicious but only very much amused. The doctor groaned. Gyuri's great body trembled, his arms shook, but he did not make a single voluntary movement. He saw the revolver in Muller's hand and felt the keen grey eyes resting on him in pitiless calm.

"And now tell us about the pastor?" said the detective in a firm clear voice.

"Oh, he was a dear, good gentleman," said No. 302 with an expression of pitying sorrow on his face. "I owed him much gratitude; that's why I put the roses in his hand."

"Yes, but you murdered him first."

"Of course, Gyuri told me to."

"And why?"

"He hated the pastor, for the old gentleman had no confidence in him."

"Is this true?" Muller turned to the doctor.

"I did not notice it," said Orszay with a voice that showed deep sorrow.

"And you?" Muller's eyes bored themselves into the orbs of the young giant, now dulled with fear.

Gyuri started and shivered. "He looked at me sharply every now and then," he murmured.

"And that was why he was killed?"

The warder's head sank on his breast.

"No, not only for that reason," continued No. 302. "Gyuri needed money again. He ordered me to bring him the silver candlesticks off the altar."

"Murder and sacrilege," said the detective calmly.

"No, I did not rob the church. When I had buried the reverend gentleman I heard the cock crowing. I was afraid I might get home here too late and I forgot the candlesticks. I had to stop to wash my hands in the brook. While I was there I saw shepherd Janci coming along and I hid behind the willows. He almost discovered me once, but Janci's a dreamer, he sees things nobody else sees — and he doesn't see things that everybody else does see. I couldn't help laughing at his sleepy face. But I didn't laugh when I came back to the asylum. Gyuri was waiting for me at the door. When he saw that I hadn't brought the candlesticks he beat me and tortured me worse than he'd ever done before."

"And you didn't tell anyone?"

"Why, no; because I was afraid that if I told on him, I'd never be able to go out again."

"And you, quite alone, could carry the pastor's body out of his room?"

"I am very strong."

"How did you arrange it that there should be no traces of blood to betray you?"

"I waited until the body had stiffened, then I tied up the wound and carried him down into the crypt."

"Why did you do that?"

"I didn't want to leave him in that horrid pool of blood."

"You were sorry for him then?"

"Why, yes; it looked so horrid to see him lying there — and he had always been so good to me. He was so good to me that very evening when I entered his study.

"He recognised you?

"Certainly. He sprang up from his chair when I came in through the passage from the church. I saw that he was startled, but he smiled at me and reached out his hand to me and said: 'What brings you here, my dear Cardillac?' And then I struck. I wanted him to die with that smile on his lips. It is beautiful to see a man die smiling, it shows that he has not been afraid of death. He was dead at once. I always kill that way — I know just how to strike and where. I killed more than a hundred people years ago in Paris, and I didn't leave one of them the time for even a sigh. I was renowned for that — I had a kind heart and a sure hand."

Muller interrupted the dreadful imaginings of the madman with a question. "You got into the house through the crypt?"

"Yes, through the crypt. I found the window one night when I was prowling around in the churchyard. When I knew that the pastor was to be the next, I cut through the window bars. Gyuri went into the church one day when nobody was there and found out that it was easy to lift the stone over the entrance to the crypt. He also learned that the doors from the church to the vestry were never locked. I knew how to find the passageway, because I had been through it several times on my visits to the rectory. But it was a mere chance that the door into the pastor's study was unlocked."

"A chance that cost the life of a worthy man," said the detective gravely.

Varna nodded sadly. "But he didn't suffer, he was dead at once."

"And now tell me what this top was doing

there?" No. 302 looked at the detective in great surprise, and then laid his hand on the latter's arm. "How did you know that I had the top there?" he asked with a show of interest.

"I found its traces in the room, and it was those traces that led me here to you," answered Muller.

"How strange!" remarked Varna. "Are you like shepherd Janci that you can see the things others don't see?"

"No, I have not Janci's gift. It would be a great comfort to me and a help to the others perhaps if I had. I can only see things after they have happened."

"But you can see more than others — the others did not see the traces of the top?"

"My business is to see more than others see," said Muller. "But you have not told me yet what the top was doing there. Why did you take a toy like that with you when you went out on such an errand?"

"It was in my pocket by chance. When I reached for my handkerchief to quench the flow of blood the top came out with it. I must have touched the spring without knowing it, for the top began to spin. I stood still and watched it, then I ran after it. It spun around the room and finally came back to the body. So did I. The pastor was quite still and dead by that time."

"You have heard everything, Dr. Orszay?" asked the detective, rising from his chair.

"Yes, I have heard everything," answered the venerable head of the asylum. He was utterly crushed by the realisation that all this tragedy and horror had gone out from his house.

Varna rose also. He understood perfectly that now Gyuri's power was at an end and he was as pleased as a child that has just received a present. "And now you're going to shoot him?" he asked, in the tone a boy would use if asking when the fireworks were to begin.

Muller shook his head. "No, my dear Cardillac," he replied gravely. "He will not be shot — that is a death for a brave soldier — but this man has deserved — " He did not finish the sentence, for the warder sank to the floor unconscious.

"What a coward!" murmured the detective scornfully, looking down at the giant frame that lay prostrate before him. Even in his wide experience he had known of no case of a man of such strength and such bestial cruelty, combined with such utter cowardice.

Varna also stood looking down at the unconscious warder. Then he glanced up with a cunning smile at the other two men who stood there. The doctor, pale and trembling with horror, covered his face with his hands. Muller turned to the door to call in the attendants waiting outside. During the moment's pause that ensued the madman bent over his worktable, seized a knife that lay there and dropped on one knee beside the prostrate form. His hand was raised to strike when a calm voice said: "Fie! Cardillac, for shame! Do not belittle yourself. This man here is not worthy of your knife, the hangman will look after him."

Varna raised his loose-jointed frame and looked about with glistening eyes and trembling lips. His mind was completely darkened once more. "I must kill him — I must have his blood — there is no one to see me," he murmured. "I am a hangman too — he has made a hangman of me," and again he bent with uplifted hand over the man who had utilised his terrible misfortune to make a criminal of him. But two of the waiting attendants seized his arms and threw him back on the floor, while the other two carted Gyuri out. Both unfortunates were soon securely guarded.

"Do not be angry with me, doctor," said Muller gravely, as he walked through the garden accompanied by Orszay.

Doctor Orszay laughed bitterly. "Why should I be angry with you — you who have discovered my inexcusable credulity?"

"Inexcusable? Oh, no, doctor; it was quite natural that you should have believed a man who had himself so well in hand, and who knew so well how to play his part. When we come to think of it, we realise that most crimes have been made possible through some one's credulity, or over-confidence, a credulity which, in the light of subsequent events, seems quite incomprehensible. Do not reproach yourself and do not lose heart. Your only fault was that you did not recognise the heart of the beast of prey in this admirable human form."

"What course will the law take?" asked Orszay. "The poor unfortunate madman — whose knife took all these lives — cannot be held responsible, can he?"

"Oh, no; his misfortune protects him. But as for the other, though his hands bear no actual bloodstains, he is more truly a murderer than the unhappy man who was his tool. Hanging is too good for him. There are times when even I could wish that we were back in the Middle Ages, when it was possible to torture a prisoner."

"You do not look like that sort of a man," smiled the doctor through his sadness.

"No, I am the most good-natured of men usually, I think — the meekest anyway," answered Muller. "But a case like this — . However, as I said before, keep a stout heart, doctor, and do not waste time in unnecessary self-reproachings." The detective pressed the doctor's hand warmly and walked down the hill towards the village.

He went at once to the office of the magistrate and made his report, then returned to the rectory and packed his grip. He arranged for its transport to the railway station, as he himself preferred to walk the inconsiderable distance. He passed through the village and had just entered the open fields when he met Janci with his flock. The shepherd hastened his steps when he saw the detective approaching.

"You have found him, sir?" he exclaimed as he came up to Muller. The men had come to be friends by this time. The silent shepherd with the power of second sight had won Muller's interest at once.

"Yes, I found him. It is Gyuri, the warder at the asylum."

"No, sir, it is not Gyuri — Gyuri did not do it."

"But when I tell you that he did?"

"But I tell you, sir, that Gyuri did not do it. The man who did it — he has yellowish hands — I saw them — I saw big yellowish hands. Gyuri's hands are big, but they are brown."

"Janci, you are right. I was only trying to test you. Gyuri did not do it; that is, he did not do it with his own hands. The man who held the knife that struck down the pastor was Varna, the crazy mechanician."

Janci beat his forehead. "Oh, I am a foolish and useless dreamer!" he exclaimed; "of course it was Varna's hands that I saw. I have seen them a hundred times when he came down into the village, and yet when I saw them in the vision I did not recognise them."

"We're all dreamers, Janci — and our dreams are very useless generally."

"Yours are not useless, sir," said the shepherd. "If I had as much brains as you have, my dreams might be of some good."

Muller smiled. "And if I had your visions, Janci, it would be a powerful aid to me in my profession."

"I don't think you need them, sir. You can find out the hidden things without them. You are going to leave us?"

"Yes, Janci, I must go back to Budapest, and from there to Vienna. They need me on another case."

"It's a sad work, this bringing people to the gallows, isn't it?"

"Yes, Janci, it is sometimes. But it's a good thing to be able to avenge crime and bring justice to the injured. Good-bye, Janci."

"Good-bye, sir, and God speed you."

The shepherd stood looking after the small, slight figure of the man who walked on rapidly through the heather. "He's the right one for the work," murmured Janci as he turned slowly back towards the village.

An hour later Muller stood in the little waiting-room of the railway station writing a telegram. It was addressed to Count — — .

"Do you know the shepherd Janci? It would be a good thing to make him the official detective for the village. He has high qualifications for the profession. If I had his gifts combined with my own, not one could escape me. I have found this one however. The guards are already taking him to you. My work here is done. If I should be needed again I can be found at Police Headquarters, Vienna.

"Respectfully,
"JOSEPH MULLER."

While the detective was writing his message — it was one of the rare moments of humour that Muller allowed himself, and he wondered mildly what the stately Hungarian nobleman would think of it — a heavy farm wagon jolted over the country roads towards the little county seat. Sitting beside the driver and riding about the wagon were armed peasants. The figure of a man, securely bound, his face distorted by rage and fear, lay in the wagon. It was Gyuri Kovacz, who had murdered by the hands of another, and who was now on his way to meet the death that was his due.

And at one of the barred windows in the big yellow house stood a sallow-faced man, looking out at the rising moon with sad, tired eyes. His lips were parted in a smile like that of a dreaming child, and he hummed a gentle lullaby.

In his compartment of the express from Budapest to Vienna, Joseph Muller sat thinking over the strange events that had called him to the obscure little Hungarian village. He had met with many strange cases in his long career, but this particular case had some features which were unique. Muller's lips set hard and his hands tightened to fists as he murmured: "I've met with criminals who used strange tools, but never before have I met with one who had the cunning and the incredible cruelty to utilise the mania of an unhinged human mind. It is a thousand times worse than those criminals who, now and then throughout the ages, have trained brute beasts to murder for them. Truly, this Hungarian peasant, Gyuri Kovacz, deserves a high place in the infamous roll-call of the great criminals of history. A student of crime might almost be led to think that it is a pity his career has been cut short so soon. He might have gone far.

"But for humanity's sake" (Muller's eyes gleamed), "I am thankful that I was able to discover this beast in human form and render him innocuous; he had done quite enough."